Clementine's Letter

Clementine's Letter

SARA PENNYPACKER

PICTURES BY
Marla Frazee

SCHOLASTIC INC.
New York Toronto London Auckland Sydney
Mexico City New Delhi Hong Kong Buenos Aires

ISBN-13: 978-0-545-15946-3
ISBN-10: 0-545-15946-6

Text copyright © 2008 by Sara Pennypacker. Illustrations copyright © 2008 by Marla Frazee. All rights reserved. Published by Scholastic Inc., 557 Broadway, New York, NY 10012, by arrangement with Hyperion Books for Children, an imprint of Disney Children's Book Group, LLC. SCHOLASTIC and associated logos are trademarks and/or registered trademarks of Scholastic Inc.

12 11   13 14/0

Printed in the U.S.A.   40

First Scholastic printing, March 2009

This book is set in 15-point Fournier.
The illustrations for this book were done with pen and ink on Strathmore paper.

Many thanks to Grace McAllister for her drawings on pages 41 and 45, and for her handwriting on pages 40, 48, 76, 77, 86, 87, 100, 101, 121, and 129. And thanks to her parents for their handwriting contributions on pages 48, 76, 87, 100, 101, and 119.

For my kids, Hilly and Caleb, who opened their hearts so that Clementine's would beat.

—S.P.

This makes three clementines for my big brother, Mark Frazee, the produce guru.

—M.F.

"I pledge allegiance to the flag of the United States of . . . *ouch*!"

There is a lot of poking that goes on in third grade. It was Norris-Boris-Morris. "Horace," he whispered.

"I'll think about it," I whispered back.

Norris-Boris-Morris's name is really Norris. I know that *now*. But in the beginning of the year, I used to call him all three "Orris" names because I could never remember which one was his. He liked that. And now he's always trying to get me to add another one. Last week he tried for Glorris, but

I said No. It has to be a real name.

"Okay," I said after the pledge. "Norris-Boris-Morris-Horace."

My teacher caught my eye and tugged on his ear. This is our secret code for Time to Be Listening. So I sat up and listened to him, even though it was just "Raise your hand if you're absent" and "Who's got milk money?" stuff.

But right after that, it got interesting.

"Clementine, would you please go to Principal Rice's office to get her."

Whenever my teacher needs someone to run an errand to the principal's office, he sends me. This is because I am so responsible. Okay, fine, it's also because I get sent so often I could find my way with my eyes closed.

Which I tried once. You'd be amazed at how many bruises you can get from just one water fountain.

When I got to Principal Rice's office, she stuck out her hand for a note from my teacher to tell her what the problem was.

"Nope, no little chats today!" I told her. "Today I'm just here to bring you back to our classroom."

"Oh, right," she said. "It's time."

As we walked down the hall, I reminded her that I hadn't been sent to her office for a little chat on Friday, either. "Did you miss me? My teacher said

I had a red-letter day. He said I was really getting the hang of third grade."

"I did notice you didn't come in, Clementine," Mrs. Rice said. "In fact, I heard you had a very successful week. Congratulations. Your teacher said you and he were really in sync these days."

"In sink?"

"In sync. It means you work well together. You understand each other."

Back in the classroom my teacher sat down at his desk and let Mrs. Rice take over, because she is the boss of him. But he was smiling. Mrs. Rice was smiling, too, when she said, "Class, we have some news to tell you." This tricked me into thinking it was good news.

"As I'm sure you all know," she went on, "your teacher has a special interest in ancient Egypt."

We knew that, all right. Mummies and sphinxes and pyramids were scattered all over the classroom,

and for the past month, everything had been *Egypt this* and *Egypt that*.

Which I was glad about. My last year's teacher had been nuts about Ye Olden Prairie Days. This would have been okay except she only liked *inside* stuff . . . making bonnets and cooking johnnycakes. I wanted to do some Ye Olden Prairie Days *outside* stuff, like lassoing buffalo and digging for gold and catching outlaws drinking beer in saloons. But my last year's teacher said, Nope, it was bonnets and johnnycakes and sitting in your seat all day. Besides, she said, all that other stuff was from Ye Olden Wild West Days. Just *remembering* how boring last year was practically made me fall asleep.

But I didn't, because I wanted to know what the good news was.

"When I learned that this year's Adventures for Teachers program was an archaeological dig in Egypt," the principal continued, "I nominated your teacher." Mrs. Rice looked proud of herself, but I didn't see what was so great yet. "And I am delighted to tell you that over the weekend, we learned Mr. D'Matz is a finalist!"

When Principal Rice said our teacher's name, all the kids sucked in their breath at the same time. This is because "D'Matz" is almost a swear. Actually, it's almost *two* swears. If you say the first part wrong, it could sound like a word that also means a wall that holds back water. If you say the second part wrong, it could sound like a word that also means a donkey. But no one would think you meant those words.

On the first day of school, I was trying so hard not to make a mistake with either part of his name that I made a mistake about both parts. I am not even kidding about that.

At recess, I apologized and explained that I only said his name wrong because I was so worried about saying his name wrong. Mr. D'Matz said he understood and besides, it was bound to happen one day.

But since then, all the kids just call him

"Teacher." We aren't taking any chances.

I guess Mrs. Rice didn't care about making a mistake. She probably thought, *So what if I get sent to the principal's office? I live there!*

"Mr. D'Matz will be leaving after lunch today—he'll spend the week with the Adventures for Teachers Committee. But we'll see him again on Friday at the statehouse. There'll be a ceremony there to name the winning teacher, and we're invited. Then, if he's chosen, Mr. D'Matz will fly off to Egypt for the big adventure."

We all sucked in our breath again when she said his name, and so I almost missed what she said next. But I heard it: "Which means he will be gone for the rest of the year."

Mrs. Rice went on talking, but my ears were so full of *gone for the rest of the year* that I couldn't hear anything else.

I looked over at my teacher. I waited for him to

jump up and say, "Nope, sorry, Mrs. Rice. I can't go away for the rest of the year because I promised to be here. I stood right in front of my students and said, 'I will be your teacher this year.' It's still this year, so I have to stay and be their teacher. I won't break my promise."

But he didn't do that. He just sat at his desk smiling at Mrs. Rice!

"This is a Tremendous Opportunity," Principal Rice was saying in her capital-letters voice. "We should all be very proud of Mr. D'Matz."

All the kids clapped and made faces like they were happy about the Tremendous Opportunity and proud of our teacher.

Not me. I don't think breaking a promise is a reason to be proud of someone.

CHAPTER
2

When we lined up for lunch, my teacher said, "Good-bye, see you all Friday!"

All the kids said, "Good-bye, see you Friday," except me. My mouth made the words, but my voice wasn't working.

I guess my feet weren't working either. Everybody left, and I was stuck standing at the door.

"Yes, Clementine?" my teacher asked. "Is everything all right?"

"Of course," I said. Except my voice still wasn't working right because it came out sounding exactly like "No!"

"No?" my teacher asked. "Want to tell me what's wrong?"

"How come you didn't tell us? How come on Friday you said, 'See you next week'?"

"I didn't know then. Principal Rice nominated me in secret. Those were the rules," he said.

"Well, what about all the things you said we were going to do this year? What about Fraction Blasters? What about our Weather-Across-the-World project? What about Friend of the Week?"

"I'll leave my lesson plans for the substitute. You'll do them with her."

"But you said *we'll* do them."

"You don't need me to learn those things."

"But what about me getting the hang of third grade? What about us working well together in the sink these days?"

Mr. D'Matz leaned back in his chair. "Oh," he said. "I see. Clementine, I think you are getting the hang of third grade. All by yourself. I think you'd be successful with any teacher."

I gave him a look that said I'd heard that joke before and it was N-O-T, *not* funny.

"Really," he said. "And it's part of my job to know when students are ready for things. Do you remember the story about the mother bird and the baby birds?"

I did, because it was his favorite story. Whenever he would start to tell it, all the kids would make secret here-we-go-again faces at each other. Since there were no other kids there, I made the face inside myself when Mr. D'Matz started.

"The mother bird lays her eggs and takes very good care of them. She sits on them until they hatch and then she keeps them warm and feeds them in the nest," he said.

Everybody knows about that part—the nice part. It's the end part that's so bad.

"And then one day, after the babies have been sitting on the branch outside the nest for a while, do you know what the mother bird does?"

"Yes, I do," I said. "*Whack!* Out of the blue, she kicks them off the branch. I think there should be a bird jail for mothers like that."

"But she has to do that. If she doesn't push them off the branch that first time, they'll never know they can fly. The mother bird knows when they're ready."

"Well, I still don't think she should do it. I think she should say, 'Hey, kids, some day *when you feel like it*, just flap your wings like this.' And then they can say, 'Not today, thanks,' if they want to."

"And you're saying, 'Not today, thanks,' about my leaving the class?"

I looked out the window and made my mouth into a ruler line so it wouldn't say, "No, I'm saying, 'Not *this year*, thanks,' about that."

Mr. D'Matz sighed and nodded to my lunch box.

"Why don't you head on down to the cafeteria before lunch is over. When you get back, Mrs. Nagel will be here. I think you'll feel better when you meet her."

Sure enough, when we came back, a lady in a green dress was sitting in my teacher's chair. She was unpacking a big bag.

I went up to her desk to watch.

She put an "I ♥ HOMEROOM" mug where my teacher usually kept his TEA IS 4 TEACHERS mug.

Then out came a package of YOU'RE A STAR! stickers.

A tissue box with buttons and shells glued onto it.

A framed photo of a pink rat wrapped in a blue blanket.

Wait a minute. I picked up the photo for a closer look. Its tail and paws were hidden by the blanket and it was hard to see the whiskers, but that's what it was all right: a pink rat in a blue blanket. This substitute might not be so bad after all.

The substitute took the picture from me and asked what my name was. I told her, and then she said, "Well, Clementine, shouldn't you be at your desk?"

"Not yet," I told her. "Our teacher lets us visit until twelve thirty."

"Well, I'm your teacher now. So why don't you go find your seat?"

So I had to walk back to my desk with

everybody looking at me, which I hate.

The substitute stood up and clapped her hands. "Good afternoon, students! My name is Mrs. Nagel." Then she went over to the board and wrote her name in big letters right next to our real teacher's name. As if it belonged there!

She turned around and clapped her hands again. "The first thing we're going to do today," she said, "is make Mr. D'Matz a good luck card."

She took a stack of folded sheets of paper and

handed them out. When we each had one, she said, "Don't make a mark on it yet."

I crossed out the picture of outlaws drinking beer in a saloon I had already drawn. My teacher calls me "Quick-draw McGraw" sometimes. He knows to give the "Don't make a mark on it" rule *before* he passes out the paper. This substitute was going to be a lot of trouble.

Mrs. Nagel told us to write "Good Luck!"

inside our cards, and when everyone was finished, she said we could draw a picture on the outside. "Something that will make him feel lucky!"

Next to me, Lilly started to draw her usual: tulips under a rainbow. In front of her, her twin brother, Willy, was starting his usual, too: a zombie shark with long pointy teeth.

I used to be afraid of pointy things. I'm not anymore.

Okay, fine, I still am.

Lilly leaned over to poke his neck. "Willy," she reminded him, "he's probably a nervous wreck worrying about whether he's going to win. It's supposed to be something to make him feel *lucky*."

Willy shrugged. "Zombie sharks make me feel lucky," he said. He added a few more teeth.

I am such a good artist that I don't have a "usual." I can draw anything. So I took out my markers and tried to think of something lucky to draw for my teacher. And for the first time in my life, all I could think of was . . . NOTHING.

I just sat there looking at my scribbled-over drawing of outlaws and my no-ideas hand until I felt a poke in my side.

"Brontosaurus," Norris-Boris-Morris-Horace whispered.

I almost said No, it has to be a real name. But

then I thought: well, I have a name that's a fruit, so why can't someone have a name that's a dinosaur? "Okay," I whispered back. "Norris-Boris-Morris-Horace-Brontosaurus. But that's it. Only one dinosaur name. No stegosaurus. No brachiosaurus."

"Clementine?" Mrs. Nagel had sneaked up on me. "Are you and Norris having a lesson on dinosaurs? Because you need to be working on your Good Luck cards."

I felt my ears get so hot and embarrassed I thought my hair was going to catch fire.

At recess, Norris apologized for getting me in trouble. "Are you mad at me?"

"No," I told him. "I'm mad at *her*. And our teacher. He shouldn't have left."

"He probably couldn't help it," Norris said. "Mrs. Rice probably made him."

"You're right! She's the boss of him, so he probably had to say yes! And you know how he

was always saying how much he enjoyed being with us? Well, he's probably missing us right now!"

"Yep," said Norris. "Probably."

Suddenly I felt a lot better. "Hey," I said. "How about Doris?"

Norris-Boris-Morris-Horace-Brontosaurus thought about that for a while, and then he sighed. "I don't know," he said. "I'm not sure a girl's name is a good idea. It's been hard enough being stuck with Norris."

When we came in from afternoon recess, I saw a good surprise: a paper plate with an apple slice on each desk. Mrs. Nagel was probably trying to make up for how mean she'd been. I didn't think an apple slice was enough, but it was a start.

But then I saw a bad surprise, too. Zippy and Bump were lying in their cage. Not moving. I had never seen this before. Then I remembered something: on Monday mornings, first thing, Mr. D'Matz picked a Hamster Helper for the week. The Hamster Helper's job was to give Zippy and Bump food and water right away, since on Fridays we only left them enough to last the weekend.

Mr. D'Matz hadn't picked a Hamster Helper. He'd forgotten about his promise to them, too. And now it was Monday *afternoon.*

I ran over to the cage and filled their food tray and water bottle. I patted Zippy and Bump while they ate and told them how sorry I was that we forgot them. They still seemed kind of skinny, so I got my apple slice and put it in their cage.

"Clementine, you need to take your seat now,"

Mrs. Nagel yelled. Okay, fine, I guess she didn't yell it. But it made my ears hurt just the same. "And where is your science experiment?"

"My science experiment?"

"I left a slice of apple on each desk. We're going to do a science experiment with it. Yours is gone."

"I thought it was a present," I explained. "I gave it to Zippy and Bump. They were almost dead because we hadn't fed them today."

Mrs. Nagel was probably mad I'd thought of this good reason, because she said, "I'm sorry. There aren't any more apples. You'll have to look on with someone during the experiment."

"She can have mine," Lilly said.

"She can have mine," Willy said at almost the same time.

"She can have mine," Norris-Boris-Morris-Horace-Brontosaurus said.

I guess the class was sick of Mrs. Nagel being

mean to me, because all the kids offered me their apple slices.

But Mrs. Nagel decided, No. "It's fine. Clementine can watch the rest of us."

So I did. And let me tell you, I did not miss out on anything.

Leave a slice of apple out in the air. The apple turns brown because of oxidation. Big deal.

Just before school ended, Principal Rice came back. She went over and whispered with the substitute for a minute. Then I saw her reach for the framed picture. I listened hard for the substitute to tell Mrs. Rice to go find her seat.

But no! Instead, the substitute just smiled! "My new nephew," I heard her sigh. "Isn't he a cutie?"

I took out a marker. *NO BABIES FOR ME!* I wrote on my arm.

I like to write important reminders on my arm. That way, I don't lose them—I always know where my arm is, which is not true about pieces of paper. Plus, they look like tattoos. On Sunday nights, my mother scrubs all the week's notes off, and I start over. This was a good one to start with.

Mrs. Rice picked up a stack of papers and came to the front of the room. She didn't have to use any "Give me your attention" hand claps because all the kids' eyes were pulled to her like magnets. I might go to principal school when I grow up so I can learn that trick.

Mrs. Rice passed out the papers. My hand wanted to draw a picture on mine, but I told it to just wait.

"You're each going to write a letter to the Adventures for Teachers judges," she said. "You're going to tell them why your teacher should win the trip. Take it with you tonight for homework. I'll come back tomorrow to collect them and send them in. Now, doesn't that sound like a good idea?"

All the kids pretended this sounded like a good idea. Except me, because it was not. A good idea is something like catching outlaws drinking beer in saloons. Or a teacher sticking around to be your teacher, if that's what he promised.

On the way home, Margaret sat beside me as usual. I kept my face turned to the window, but Margaret doesn't like it when I don't look at her. She pinched me until I turned around.

"What's the matter with your eyes?" she asked. "Have you been crying?"

"No," I said. Then I turned back to the window. Margaret pinched me back to her again.

"Okay, fine," I said. "Maybe I was. A little. In the girls' room."

"How come?" she asked.

So I told her about everything that had

happened. "He promised he'd be our teacher and now he doesn't care about that. If he wins, he'll be gone for the rest of the year. I was just getting the hang of third grade and now I'll have to start all over. And Mrs. Nagel's really mean."

I felt a poke in my neck and turned around. "Mrs. Nagel isn't mean," Lilly said. "She's

nice." Then she poked her brother and said, "Willy. Tell Clementine that Mrs. Nagel's not mean."

Willy shrugged. "She's not mean," he said.

Which didn't count. Willy does everything Lilly tells him to.

Sometimes I wish I had a twin brother whose name rhymed with mine and who did everything I told him to. Instead, I have a brother who is only three years old and who does everything I tell him *not* to do.

Plus, his name doesn't rhyme with mine and it's not even a fruit name like I got stuck with. Which reminded me.

I got out a marker and wrote COLLECT MORE VEGETABLE NAMES FOR TURNIP on my arm. Then I turned back to Willy and Lilly. "She's mean *to me*. I was in trouble all day."

"That's because you were *doing* things," Lilly

said. "I didn't get into trouble today. I never get into any trouble."

"It was probably your own fault, Clementine," Margaret interrupted, although I was N-O-T, *not* talking to her. "You were probably doing weird things. You're always doing weird things. Why don't you just watch Lilly and copy her this week?"

"That sounds like a dumb idea," I said.

Willy poked my neck. "It's what I do," he told me. "And I never get into any trouble, either."

I slumped down into my seat. "Okay, fine," I said. "I'll do it."

When I got home from school, I took out my homework assignment, put it on the kitchen table and stared at the blank sheet of paper.

My mom came in and asked me if I wanted a snack.

"No," I said. I kept my teeth clenched together so it sounded like a growl. A *fierce* growl. "What I want is for my teacher not to leave."

My mom gave me some cheese and juice anyway. "Mr. D'Matz is leaving? Oh, that's too bad. You like him a lot. Want to tell me about it?"

Just then we heard a crash from the living room

and my brother laughing. This meant he was in the art supply cupboard again.

"Let's hope he didn't find those markers!" My mom ran out of the room.

Then my dad walked in. He took one look at my face and unhooked the keys from his belt. "Do you want to take a ride?" he asked.

When I'm angry, my dad lets me ride the service elevator until I calm down.

"No," I growled again. "What I want is to not have to do this homework."

My dad sat down beside me. "Tough assignment, huh? Want to tell me about it?" he asked. I really did. But just then his work phone rang. When he came back, he said, "Sorry, Sport, it'll have to wait. The elevator's broken again. We'll talk about it later."

My dad is the manager of our apartment building. He says this means he's in charge of all the problems. But he's in charge of all the good parts, too.

Like the roof. Sometimes, on summer nights, my family goes up to the rooftop, which is eight stories high. We can see all of Boston from there. We bring up a large extra-cheese pizza and a lamp with a really long extension cord, and we all play the board game Life up there on top of the city. Well, my parents and I play Life—Broccoli just jams the pegs into the little plastic cars and races them around the board. This makes my parents laugh—they say my brother is living Life in the fast lane.

Just then my kitten walked into the kitchen and jumped onto my lap. I cuddled him and fed him pieces of my cheese. He started to purr.

"Don't worry, *I'm* not going to go off anywhere," I told him. "Nope, you can count on me. If *I* say I'm going to be here, I'm going to be here, Moisturizer."

My brother came into the kitchen then. "Play with me!"

I held up my paper. "I can't, Lima Bean. I have to do my homework." My brother laughed as if I'd told him a really good joke and climbed up onto my lap next to Moisturizer.

"It's not funny," I told him. "You'll see. In five years, you'll be in third grade like I am, and then you might have to do a stupid assignment like this one."

I'm actually not so sure about this. When my brother wakes up, he sticks one foot up in the air

and smiles really big when he sees it—as if it's his best friend he's been missing all night. He waggles it back and forth and thinks it's waving to him. "Hi, foot!" he yells. Then he does the same thing with his other foot.

I do not think anyone who says hello to his own feet is ever going to make it to third grade.

I guess my brother didn't think he was ever going to make it to third grade, either. He just meowed at me, and then he and Moisturizer took turns eating pieces of my cheese. When it was all gone, they jumped down and went off to play together.

"Dear Adventures for Teachers judges," I wrote. Then I stared at my paper and tried to think of something to say. I tried and tried until I started to smell brain smoke. Then I gave up and went to the freezer for a Popsicle to cool my head down.

While I was eating it, my dad came back in to

get a wrench. He walked past me, shaking his head. "I ought to write a book," he muttered.

My dad is always saying he ought to write a book. He says that as a building manager he sees a lot of strange things. Mostly, he says, they're fascinating, wonderful things. But he also says there are a lot more nut-balls out there than anyone could imagine. And he could write a really good book if he ever sat down to try.

Suddenly I had a wonderful idea.

I went to my mom's art supply cupboard and took out a fresh sketch pad. On the cover, in really important-looking letters, I wrote, THE BUILDING MANAGER—BY DAD. Underneath, I drew a picture of our apartment building. On the first page, I wrote the first sentence, to get him started.

Once there was a building manager.

I went into my parents' bedroom and put the pad

on the table next to my dad's side of the bed. Then I brought my homework up to the lobby to see if he could help me while he was fixing the elevator.

I didn't find him. But I did find Margaret's older brother, Mitchell. He was oiling his baseball glove, looking bored.

"What are you doing down here?" I asked.

Mitchell pointed up. "Margaret's cleaning my room. I have to stay out."

My room is a little tiny bit messy. I wondered if

I should have Margaret clean it so it looked like hers. "How much does it cost?" I asked.

"Three dollars," Mitchell answered.

"Three dollars? Oh. I guess I wouldn't pay that much just to get my room cleaned."

"Neither would I," Mitchell agreed. "That's how much Margaret pays *me* to let her do it. I'm saving up for a new bat. Otherwise I wouldn't let her. When she's done, I can't find any of my stuff."

"She hides it?"

"No, she just lines it all up in order. You know Margaret and her rules . . . short to tall, new to old, alphabetical order. It takes me hours to get it all back the way I like it again."

Mitchell slumped down and I slumped down the same way so he wouldn't feel lonely. Then I told him all about my teacher trying to go to Egypt. "That's what he thinks is more important than us! Digging around looking for old mummies and dumb

42

hieroglyphics. And he doesn't even want to go!"

"So he'll be camping," Mitchell said.

"I guess," I said. "But he'll be *gone*, Mitchell! After he promised us he'd be here all year!"

But Mitchell was stuck on the camping thing. He whistled. "I sure hope he doesn't get stuck in a tent with someone like Beans McCloud!"

"You're not listening to me!"

Mitchell kept on not listening to me. "Dude!" he said, shaking his head as if he still couldn't get over how bad things had been. "I had to live with

him for two whole weeks at summer camp!"

I gave up. "All right. What was so bad about Beans McCloud?"

"What *wasn't* so bad about him? Well, to start with . . . his socks! He never took them off, and I mean never. I think his mother put those socks on Beans in the cradle and he just got attached to them or something." Mitchell pinched his nose and pretended to faint. "Those socks nearly peeled the canvas off our tent!"

"Oh, come on," I said. "It couldn't have been that bad."

Mitchell took off his Red Sox cap and held it over his heart, which means, *I swear to the Red Sox.* "Clementine," he said, "when that kid went hiking, even the skunks keeled over."

I couldn't help laughing at that. When I have a boyfriend, which will be never, I'm going to pick someone as funny as Mitchell. I did a drawing on the back of my homework paper so I wouldn't forget what he said. Here it is:

Mitchell was still muttering about Beans. "And that was just the *first* thing. That kid should have come with a warning label!"

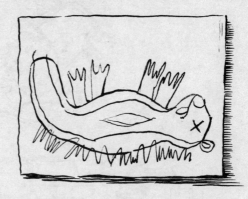

"How come?"

"So somebody would have known not to let him in!"

And suddenly I had a really good idea!

I flipped my homework paper over to the "Dear Adventures for Teachers" side. "Okay, start at the beginning," I said. "Tell me everything that should have been on Beans McCloud's warning label. Don't leave anything out."

At breakfast Tuesday morning, my mom asked about my teacher leaving.

"Oh, it's no big deal," I told her. "He'll be back on Monday."

Then my dad asked how I was coming with my homework assignment. I told him, Great. "I just need one more thing: how do you spell 'Menace to Society'?" My dad spelled it, then asked if that was really all. "I thought it was giving you some trouble."

"Nope. Mitchell helped me, and it was easy."

"That was nice of him," he said. "Do you want to show it to us?"

"Oh . . . um . . . no. It's sort of a surprise," I said. Which was the truth, because my letter was going to be a pretty big surprise to those judges, all right!

My dad left and I sneaked into his room to see if he had worked on the book I had started for him. He had. Just one sentence though. After

Once there was a building manager.

he had written:

HE WAS EXTREMELY HANDSOME AND HE HAD THE STRENGTH OF TEN OXEN.

Sometimes my dad needs help staying on track. So I pointed him in the right direction again.

He saw lots of interesting things!

I wrote.

On the bus ride to school, I told Margaret about helping him start a book.

She just snorted. "Well, now you'll have to do something nice for your mother. That's the rule. It's not fair if you don't."

"You're right," I said. "I don't like it when String Bean gets a present and I don't. And my mom lives in that room, too, so she's going to know about it."

Margaret looked like she was really mad at me then. "You're so lucky," she growled.

"What do you mean?"

"You're always so lucky and you don't even know it."

"How am I lucky, Margaret?" I was hoping she had found out I was getting a gorilla for Christmas. But it wasn't that.

"Well, for one thing, you don't have Mitchell."

"I have Zucchini," I said.

"*Your* brother's cute." She made a face that said, *You have no idea what I have to put up with!* I didn't make the face back because I happen to think Mitchell is not so bad at all. Which does N-O-T, *not* mean he is my boyfriend.

"And for another thing, you don't have Alan," she added.

Alan is Margaret's mother's boyfriend. Whenever Margaret says his name she makes a face like someone's asking her to pat a slug. I made the face back, because she's right about Alan.

I figured it was really my dad who was lucky Mom didn't have a boyfriend, but I didn't tell Margaret. Instead I just asked her if there was anything else she thought I was lucky about.

"If you don't know, I'm not going to tell you," she said. Then she slammed her mouth into a ruler line. Except it didn't work because her lips got stuck on her braces, which she calls teeth bracelets. I turned away so I wouldn't laugh, because I know how bad it feels to be laughed at.

Okay, fine. Also because she's a little bit bigger than I am and her pocketbook has pointy edges.

"Don't forget," Margaret said when we got off the bus. "Today, only do what Lilly does."

I tried.

As soon as Lilly sat down, she opened up her backpack, took her homework paper out, and put it into her desk. I opened up my backpack, took my homework paper out, and put it into my desk.

So far, so good.

Then Lilly poked her brother in the back of his neck and hissed at him to put his homework paper away, too. I poked Willy's neck—but not too hard, because he had a lot of poke marks there—and hissed at him, too.

Then Mrs. Nagel clapped her hands for our attention.

Lilly slapped her hands into a pile on her desk and straightened up. I stretched over to see better.

She was staring at Mrs. Nagel as if she was hypnotized. I slapped my hands into a pile and made the hypnotized look. Then I slid down to the floor to get a better look at what Lilly was doing with the rest of her body.

And you will not believe what I saw: every part of Lilly was completely frozen! Nothing was wiggling, not a single toe! Mrs. Nagel had hypnotized her into a statue! In front of her, Willy was frozen, too.

"Clementine, what are you doing on the floor?" Mrs. Nagel shouted. Okay, fine, maybe she just *said* it, but from the floor it sounded like a shout. "Did you lose something?"

"No, I was just trying to see what Lilly was doing so I could do it, too," I explained.

"Well, there's an empty seat up in the front row," she said. "Maybe it would be easier for you to concentrate if you moved up here."

So I had to move to the front of the room where
I had to look at her desk with all her stuff on it
where my real teacher's stuff belonged.

Then she collected our homework papers and

put them into a big envelope. She placed the envelope on her desk. And that was good, because all day long that envelope reminded me that our teacher was N-O-T, *not* going to win that Egypt prize. Nope, once the judges read my letter they were going to send him right back to our class on Monday morning. He would be our teacher for the rest of the year. Just like he wanted to be. Just like he'd promised. It made me feel a lot better.

Okay, fine, not a lot better. But a little.

When I got home from school, my parents were sitting at the kitchen table. They were staring at a stack of mail exactly the way I had stared at my homework assignment the day before. As if they couldn't believe what they had to do. This meant it was the first of the month, which is bill day in my family. I don't like bill day, because on bill day my parents say No to whatever I ask. I tried anyway.

"I need to collect some new names for Broccoli. Can one of you take me to the grocery store?"

"First of all, your brother's name isn't Broccoli. And second of all, No," they said at the same time. Then they both looked like they'd had a wonderful, sneaky idea. "Wait! Yes! I can!" they said at the same time, jumping up from the table. Then they looked at each other and all four of their shoulders sagged and they sank back down. "No, we can't," they both sighed at the same time. They went back to staring at the pile of bills.

My mom looked up. "It's Tuesday. Maybe Mitchell can take you."

On Tuesdays and Thursdays, Margaret's mother works late at the bank. Sometimes she pays Mitchell two dollars to run her errands and bring Margaret along so he can watch her at the same time. "It's not babysitting!" Margaret always yells at anyone they meet. "And I should be the one getting the two dollars to watch *him*!" Sometimes my parents pay Mitchell to run errands and not-babysit my brother and me, too.

I called the number.

"Red Sox training camp. Home of Mitchell the Mitt, future star player."

Mitchell is obsessed with the Boston Red Sox. He says they're the greatest baseball team in the history of the world. He says the only way the Red Sox could possibly be any better would be if he were on the team. Which he will be soon.

But he only answers the phone this way when his mother isn't home. Margaret and Mitchell's mother doesn't have a sense of humor. My dad says living with Margaret and her rules every day would strain anyone's sense of humor.

"Hi, Mitchell," I said. "My mom wants to know if you can not-babysit us this afternoon and we could go to a grocery store."

"Sure," he said. "Meet us in the lobby."

My mom and I strapped Cabbage into his stroller and waited by the elevator. When Margaret and Mitchell came down, my mom gave Mitchell two dollars to not-babysit us. Then she handed me some money to buy her a tube of oil paint at the art supply store.

"Permanent rose," she said.

Sometimes I get confused in the art store. All those beautiful colors and all those beautiful names of beautiful colors make me a little dizzy. Alizarin crimson, cerulean blue, cadmium lemon. I started to feel faint just thinking about them. I stuck my arm out to my mom. "Maybe you should write it down."

"Don't worry," she said. "You'll remember. Just think about your Great-Aunt Rose's hair. She has a permanent. Permanent rose."

"Permanent rose," I said. "I'll remember."

"Okay, good-bye, see you in an hour, remember

about the peanuts," she said.

My brother is allergic to peanuts. This means if he eats even one, his whole head will explode right off his neck.

Then we got going. We went to the drugstore, the dry cleaner's, and the video drop-off. The last stop was the art store.

In the paint section, hundreds of little paint

tubes, all neat and new, sat on the shelf. Margaret threw her hands up and backed away, as if the tubes of paint were just waiting to burst all over her clean clothes. Margaret doesn't even like to look at things that might get her dirty.

"Quick, run over to the paper aisle!" I told her. "Just keep staring at all those nice clean stacks of paper."

Mitchell took my brother off for a stroll around the store, and I went back to staring at the beautiful colors. Burnt sienna, manganese violet, viridian green—I started to feel a little woozy.

A clerk came over and asked if he could help me find something.

"I'd like a tube of mustache rose oil paint," I told him.

"Mustache rose?" he asked. "Are you sure you've got the right name?"

"I'm positive," I told him. "I know because my

Great-Aunt Rose has a mustache. Just a little bit. You have to look at her from the side to see it best. That's how I remembered—the paint color is about my great-aunt's hair."

Mitchell came up behind me and whispered into my ear.

"Oh," I said. "Make that a tube of permanent rose."

The clerk found the paint and we went up to the register to buy it. And there, sitting on the counter, was a big, beautiful wooden box with lots of little compartments inside. DELUXE ART SUPPLIES ORGANIZER, the sign said.

"Look, Mitchell!" I said. "This is like a little apartment building for paints and brushes and things to live in. My mom keeps her stuff in old cookie tins. My brother's always getting into them. . . . This has a lock! She would really like this. She'd like it so much she wouldn't feel

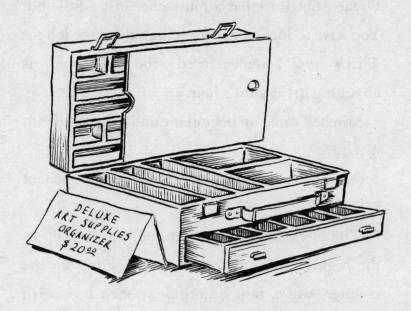

DELUXE
ART SUPPLIES
ORGANIZER
$20.00

jealous about me helping my dad write a book!"

The price tag said twenty dollars. I dug in my pockets. Two quarters and a nickel. The clerk handed me my mother's change. Three dollars and eleven cents. Probably she wouldn't mind loaning it to me for such a good present.

"Can I borrow some money?" I asked Mitchell.

"Nope," he said. "I'm saving up for a new bat, remember?"

I stared at him.

Mitchell threw his arms across his face and staggered backward. "No!" he moaned. "Not stingray eyes! Anything but that!"

My stingray eyes are extremely powerful. I use them only in emergencies. I turned them up to high power.

"Aaaauuurrrggghhhh! I give up!" Mitchell cried. He took out his money: my mom's two regular dollar bills and two brand-new ones. Margaret and Mitchell's mother works in a bank. She exchanges all her dollar bills for clean, never-been-spent money so Margaret doesn't have to worry about germs.

Now I had seven dollars and sixty-six cents. "Margaret," I yelled. "Come over here, please."

Margaret came over, squint-eyeing me.

63

"How much money do you have?" I asked.

"A dollar," she answered. "I'm going to buy some hand sanitizer."

"Not anymore, you're not. I'll give it back to you soon, but I have to buy this for my mom. You said so yourself. So she won't be jealous of the nice thing I did for my dad."

Margaret pinched her fingers around her pocketbook and shook her head. I turned my stingray eyes on her. But she just turned hers back on me. Sometimes I wish I'd never taught Margaret stingray eyes. Luckily, I never taught her high power, so I turned that on, and finally she gave up and handed over her brand-new, never-spent dollar bill.

Eight dollars and sixty-six cents. "I still need eleven dollars and thirty-four cents," I told everybody.

"I don't know how you do that, Clementine,"

Mitchell said. "You're amazing." Then he pushed the stroller toward the door. "Come on. Let's go."

"All right." I patted the art box. "Don't sell it yet, okay?" I said to the clerk. "Because I'm coming back."

CHAPTER
6

Outside, I reminded Mitchell that I still needed to find a grocery store. "But not a regular one," I said. "I need some *new* vegetable names."

He pointed down the street. "How about that?"

I looked, and there was a grocery store, all right. LEE'S CHINESE MARKET read the sign over the door. And out on the sidewalk were bins of vegetables! I ran down the street. I'd never seen some of these vegetables before.

"Bok choy, snow peas," I read the signs. "Daikon, bamboo shoots."

"Do you have a pen?" I asked Mitchell when

67

everyone caught up to me. "I want to write down some names."

Mitchell didn't have anything in his pockets except a baseball.

I didn't bother asking Margaret, because she never carries anything with her that might leak out over her clothes.

So we went inside. I was just about to ask the grocer for a pen when my amazing corner-eyes spotted something. I ran over.

And you will not believe what I saw. Eels in a tank. Eels and eels and eels. The eels were swimming around, making knots and loops in the water, tying themselves all up and then untying themselves like magic.

"Wow," I said.

"Wow," Mitchell said.

"Wow," Bok Choy said.

"I'm going to throw up," Margaret said.

"They're just fish, Margaret," I told her. "They can't help it if they're extra long and slippery."

But Margaret had turned kind of green. "Quick!" I told her. "Run over there into the rice aisle. Just keep looking at all those bins of nice clean rice." Margaret ran away and I turned back to those eels.

Sometimes, on hot summer days, I like to make water paintings on the sidewalk in our back alley.

How you make them is this: take a nice big paint-brush, dip it in water, then paint swirly lines on the cement. The swirly lines evaporate almost as fast as you can make them, so they almost look like they're moving. Just like these eels.

Oh—I forgot to say: ask your mother first about using her paintbrush.

I pointed to the littlest one hiding in the corner. "Look how sad he looks."

"Eels can't look sad," Mitchell said. "They're eels."

"He's crying," I said. "It's just harder to tell underwater."

Mitchell made a face, but I saw him corner-eye the tank to see if it was true.

"Special: five dollars and ninety-nine cents a pound," I read the sign. "That's a pretty good price for a pet," I said.

"This isn't a pet shop, Clementine," Mitchell said.

"This is a grocery store. These eels are for eating."

"Shhh," I hissed at Mitchell for saying that in front of them.

Mitchell shrugged. "Well, it's true. People eat them. Or smoke them."

Margaret must have been listening from the rice aisle because we heard her yell, "Don't let Alan hear about this! That pipe of his is disgusting enough."

A very small, secret part of me wanted to see someone smoking an eel. But not today. And not these eels. I went up to the counter.

"Excuse me," I said to the grocer. "Can I borrow a pen?"

The grocer gave me one and I wrote my brother's new vegetable names on my arm. "Excuse me," I said again when I gave him back the pen. "Is your name Mr. Lee?"

"Yes, it is," he said.

"Well, Lee is eel spelled backward. Isn't that great? If I had a store and I was selling some things that were my name spelled backward, I'd stop selling them."

I had to stop for a minute to figure out what that would be. "Yep, if I had a store with some 'Enitnemelc's, I'd give them away as pets."

Mr. Lee just laughed, as if I'd told him a good joke.

"See?" Margaret hissed in my ear. "He thinks you're weird. You're always doing weird things, Clementine."

I icicle-eyed Margaret and left, pushing Bamboo Shoot in his stroller.

Margaret followed me. She pointed to the names on my arm. "That's weird, too," she said.

I turned to Mitchell. "Do you think so? Do you think I do weird things?"

"Of course," he said. "That's why I let you hang around with me."

Which he said because he was trying to be my boyfriend. I didn't tell him I don't want a boyfriend, because I didn't want to crack his heart like in the movies. So instead, I asked him if he had any ideas about how I could earn twenty dollars for my mom's present. He only came up with one: he could become a famous baseball player and get rich and then give me that much. I told him Thank you, but that would take too long.

When I got back home, my mom was sitting at her drawing table. I pulled her change and the tube of permanent rose from my pocket.

She held up her hands, which were covered with pastel dust. "Could you put it away for me?"

I opened the cookie tin my mom uses for oil paints. All the tubes were jumbled up together—it looked beautiful to me, but it didn't look anything like the shelves at the art store. I suddenly realized something: the art store person had put all the paints in order according to a rule. Not a dumb rule, like one of Margaret's, but a good one. "Want me to arrange these in color wheel order?" I asked.

"That would be nice, honey!" Mom said.

So I laid out all the tubes of paint in a rainbow circle, just like they'd been at the art store. When I was finished Mom leaned over and took a look. "That's wonderful," she said. "Now I won't waste time looking for a certain color. Could you do this for my watercolors and my colored pencils, too?"

"Really?" I asked. "I can touch all your stuff?"

"Sure."

"Even the special markers?"

My mom looked at me for a minute, and I could see her thinking about the time I'd colored Margaret's head with them.

"Sure. I know you know the rules about my art supplies now. So any time you feel like straightening up my things, you can go ahead."

So I put all her stuff in color wheel order, and I secret-smiled all the time, thinking about how happy she was going to be when I gave her that deluxe art supplies organizer box.

After that, I went into my parents' room to see how my dad was coming with his book. Under

He saw lots of interesting things!

he had written:

Also, he had a gorgeous wife
AND TWO REMARKABLE children.

I flipped the pad to see if he'd written any more about the interesting things on the next page. Nope. So it was up to me.

One day the building manager saw something extra interesting!

I wrote.

Then I went to put the stroller back into the storage room. On the way, I passed the trash-and-recycling room. And in there, I saw something that really *was* extra interesting: the solution to my deluxe art supplies organizer twenty dollar problem!

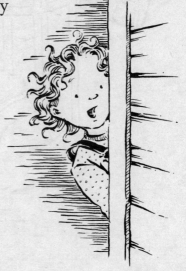

"Clementine, that's the third time I've found you staring at the clock today," Mrs. Nagel said Wednesday morning. "Are you waiting for something to happen?"

I felt my ears begin to burn. Mrs. Nagel kept looking at me. So even though I did *not* want to say what I was doing, I did.

"I'm just playing Beat the Clock," I said.

"How do you play?" Joe asked.

"I look at the clock, and then I look away and count the seconds and then look back to see how close I was. I'm getting really good. If I ever go on a game show where you have to guess how many seconds have gone by, I'm going to win. And I won't pick the dumb prizes, let me tell you."

"All right," said Mrs. Nagel. "I think that's enough of that."

But it wasn't enough. Everyone started to play Beat the Clock. Kids shouted, "Just two seconds off!" and "Eighteen seconds, I guessed it exactly!" and "You did not, I saw you peek at your watch!" until finally Mrs. Nagel taped a piece of construction paper over the clock.

The back of her head sent me a look that said, *Your teacher's going to hear about this!*

I didn't send her a look back, but if I had, it would have said, *Good, because my teacher understands about Beat the Clock. He understands about how counting with one part of my mind helps me pay attention to him with the other. We have a little arrangement about that. And besides, if my teacher wanted to tell me to stop looking at the clock he wouldn't have done it in front of the whole class. He would have held up his fingers to make a capital P for "in private." Then I would have gone up to his desk and he would have talked to me there. And I miss my teacher a lot right now. So it's a good thing he won't be gone much longer.* Which was too much to fit into a single look, anyway.

The rest of the morning got worse. By the time the recess bell rang, I bet I heard a hundred "Clementine-pay-attention!"s. And every time, I *was* paying attention!

But okay, fine, not to Mrs. Nagel, because she had gone from boring to extra-boring. Instead, I was paying attention to the astoundishing idea that had jumped into my head when I passed by the trash-and-recycling area last night. Which was the opposite of boring, believe me.

"Twenty dollars, coming soon!" I wrote on my math paper.

After a hundred hours, school was over. The bus ride took three hundred more hours. All everybody wanted to talk about was how nice Mrs. Nagel was, which showed that she had hypnotized everyone except me. Finally I was home.

My mom was just about to leave with Bean Sprout to go to story hour at the library. She handed me a cup of yogurt and an apple. The apple reminded me about Monday's science experiment, which made me feel a little bit bad. I stuffed it into my pocket.

My mom leaned over to get a closer look at the back of my neck. "Oh, for heaven's sake!" she said. Then she looked at my arms. "I'm going to have a talk with Margaret's mother."

"They're not all pinch marks," I said. "Some of them are poke marks. The neck ones came from Lilly. My right side came from Norris-Boris-Morris and my left arm—"

"A child is not a pincushion. Don't they teach that in your school?"

"It's okay. I sit in front of Joe and Maria now. Joe's too short to reach over his desk and Maria is a weak little pickle." And then I thought of something. "Wait. Now that I think about it, Maria has extra-hard fingers. Pointy, too. And what if Joe uses his pencil? He might get me in the lungs or something. I guess I'd better not go to school for a while . . . like until Monday. . . ."

"Don't be silly. I'll just write a note. . . . What did you say your substitute's name is?"

"No, Mom, don't!"

"Why not?"

"You'll just make it worse."

"Make what worse?"

So I had to tell her about all the trouble I was having with Mrs. Nagel. And about Margaret's idea about doing what Lilly did, which didn't work, and having to move.

My mom sat down beside me. "Well, I don't think that was very good advice anyway," she said. "It's never a good idea to do something just because somebody else is

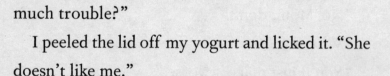

doing it. So why do you think you're having so much trouble?"

I peeled the lid off my yogurt and licked it. "She doesn't like me."

"Oh, that can't be true!" my mom said. Which she had to say because she's my mother. "There must be another reason. If you could figure it out, maybe you could fix things."

My mom grabbed Water Chesnut as he ran by and tried to put on his jacket. I watched for a while, but she wasn't getting anywhere. "He's playing Spaghetti Boy," I explained. "Be Tree Boy," I told him. "Make Branch Arms." My brother got fooled by this and my mom got his jacket on.

She zipped him up. "Thanks, Clementine. See what I mean? Sometimes you have to figure out the problem before you can figure out the solution."

That sounded like a good thing to remember, so I wrote it on my arm. My mom picked up my brother and carried him to the door because he was still being a tree. "Your father's out back. The masons are here—they're starting the new brick garden wall. Do you want to go watch them?"

I dropped my spoon. I'd been waiting all month for this, because I love bricks. I love how pretty the white mortar looks next to the red clay. I love how each brick is set exactly halfway over the one beneath it, so each row ends with either a full brick or a half a brick. I love how even it is, all the way to the top of the wall, even if the wall is a hundred stories high.

I love bricks so much that when my family made a gingerbread house last Christmas I made the sides of it with Dentyne gum for bricks and used frosting for mortar. It cost me two weeks allowance for all that gum, but it was worth it.

I thought about how much I wanted to watch the masons. And then I thought of my mom's present. "No thanks," I said. "I have something to do this afternoon."

Before I got going with my idea, I went to my dad's night table to see how he was coming with his book. Not so good. Under

One day the building manager saw something extra interesting!

he had written,

So he showed it to his daughter.

I picked up the pen and wrote,

This was because sometimes the building manager needed her help to stay on track.

Then I went down to the trash-and-recycling room.

Sometimes my parents watch a TV show about junk. People get together in a big room with their junk. The host, who is a junk expert, goes around to each of them and tells them how much their junk is worth. Sometimes, he says, "Oh, too bad you fixed this, because now it's not worth anything." And then the people act like they don't care and they say, "I still love my thing and that's what counts." This is because they are embarrassed about making the big mistake of fixing it.

But sometimes the host says, "Holy mackerel! This is amazing—this is an extremely valuable piece of junk and now you are rich!" And then the people clap their hands to their cheeks and make big O-mouths as if they are too stunned to speak. And then the host turns to the camera and says, "You, too, might have treasures in your attic or your basement!" and that's the end of the show.

When I'm a grown-up, I will not watch the junk show, because it is B-O-R-I-N-G, *boring*. But it did give me my astoundishing idea.

In between the garbage barrels and the recycling crates, there were a bunch of bags. And the bags were filled with . . . junk! A pipe. A yellow knitted tie. Four place mats made like little braided rugs. A china figurine of a rooster with a straw hat. Some other junky things.

So that TV host was right—I, too, had treasures in my basement!

Above the bags, there was a sign: CHARITY COLLECTION—DONATE YOUR UNWANTED ITEMS FOR A GOOD CAUSE.

Giving my mom a present was a good cause, all right.

I dragged the bags and a card table up to the lobby, and I taped a sign to the table: PRICE: WHATEVER YOU THINK IT'S WORTH.

PRICE:
WHATEVER YOU
THINK IT'S
WORTH

Mrs. Jacobi came in just as I was setting out the first thing—the set of braided place mats. "Look at these charming place mats!" she said. "Mrs. Beetleman is coming for tea this afternoon. These will look lovely with my teacups!" She gave me a dollar.

I set out the rest of the things. Mrs. Beetleman came in next. "I'm going to have tea with Mrs. Jacobi this afternoon," she told me. "I'd like to bring her a little present." She picked up the china rooster and gave me a dollar, too.

Next was the man from the sixth floor. He

bought the knitted tie. Fifty cents.

The rest of my neighbors came in, and they all bought something.

The last person to come was Alan. He picked up the pipe. "This is my lucky day!" he said. His face looked just like the junk-show host's face did when he discovered a treasure. "I lost a pipe exactly like this one last week! It was my favorite!" And then he gave me two dollars and stuffed the pipe into his pocket, still wearing the "Holy mackerel!" face.

I counted my money. . . . Twenty-two dollars! I put the card table back, and then I rode the elevator up to the fifth floor to give Margaret and Mitchell back their money from Tuesday.

Mitchell took his money and thanked me.

Margaret just looked sideways at the dollar bill I held out to her. "Where have you been keeping it?" she asked.

"Nowhere. Just in my pocket. See? It's still clean and new."

Margaret snorted. She took it with two fingers and went off to wash it.

It was too late to go to the art store, so I went outside to watch the masons work. And Margaret was right—I was lucky this week! They were just finishing up for the day, and they let me have the broken bricks and the leftover mortar!

I had a great idea. I took my apple from my pocket, ate it until I came to the seeds, and then picked a few out. I scraped a little hole in the dirt next to the new brick wall and planted the seeds. Then I built a little brick wall around the spot to protect the apple tree when it grew. And even though the bricks were broken, it looked beautiful.

I smiled, because when the tree was grown, I'd have all the apples I wanted. And I would invite everyone I knew over and I would say to them,

"Help yourself. Use some of these apples for a science experiment if you'd like. Or give some to your hamsters if they're hungry. Whatever you want to do with them is *fine*. There will always be plenty more."

Then I ran inside to get my parents so I could show them my wall.

When I got back to my apartment, my dad was on the phone. "No, I certainly did *not* give her that stuff. I didn't even know about it until just now."

He looked pretty mad. But my brick wall would cheer him up. As soon as he hung up, I asked him if he wanted to come with me to see what I'd made.

"No, I don't," he said. "I already know what you've made. A mess! I've been hearing about it for the last thirty minutes!"

"What do you mean?"

"That was Mrs. Beetleman. When she went to Mrs. Jacobi's for tea, she saw the place mats she'd given Mr. and Mrs. Heinz on their anniversary. Apparently

Mr. and Mrs. Heinz had thrown them out. Now Mrs. Beetleman isn't speaking to them."

"Oh," I said.

"That's not all," my dad went on. "Mrs. Jacobi called a few minutes ago. Mrs. Beetleman brought her a little china rooster. Mrs. Jacobi recognized it as the one she had given to the man on the sixth floor for his birthday. So she's mad at him. When he went up to her apartment to apologize, Mr. and Mrs. Heinz were there, explaining about the place mats. The man on the sixth floor was wearing a yellow tie. Which Mrs. Heinz's mother had knitted for Mr. Heinz. So now Mrs. Heinz isn't speaking to Mr. Heinz. And Mr. Heinz isn't speaking to the man on the sixth floor. Clementine, I'm afraid to ask, but how many people bought things from you?"

"Everybody," I said.

My dad smacked his forehead. "So this could

be just the beginning. And they're blaming me for it all."

"Now, Bill," my mom said. "When they calm down, they'll see that it's certainly not your fault. And it's not really Clementine's fault, either." She stopped to think for a minute. "Well, it's not *entirely* her fault. But how could she know, after all?"

My dad didn't answer.

"How about if tomorrow after school I apologize to everyone?" I asked.

"I guess that's a start, Sport," my dad said. "And you'll have to offer to buy back everything you sold."

Which was N-O-T, *not* fair. But my dad still looked pretty mad, so I couldn't tell him that.

Later that night, when I was trying not to think about how mad he looked, my dad came into my room. He sat on my bed with his book pad.

I pointed to it. "That's why I did it," I said. "I wanted to buy Mom a present so she wouldn't feel bad that I did something nice for you."

My dad looked at me for a while. Then he said, "But you've got that wrong, Sport. Mom would never feel bad because you did something nice for me."

"Margaret says it's a rule: if you do something nice for one person, you have to do something nice for the other person, too."

"It might be Margaret's rule. But it's not our rule. I'm happy when you do something nice for Mom, and she's happy when you do something nice for me. When you care about people, you *want* them to be happy. Don't you?"

I thought about that for a while and then I nodded.

My dad handed me his book.

"'Sometimes the building manager's daughter was too impulsive,'" I read. "'Sometimes she did things without thinking ahead. Without thinking of the consequences. It got her into a lot of trouble. Sometimes it even got her father in trouble.'"

I picked up my pen and took the pad.

She was really sorry about that.

I started to show it to my dad, then I pulled it
back and added an extra

really

And I thought of another thing—

So he forgave her!

My dad took the pen from me.

The Building manager knew his daughter
was sorry and since he loved her so much,
he always forgave her. But he worried
about her. He worried she might feel
bad about getting into trouble when
she was too impulsive. He hoped she
could try to think ahead more. To
think about what might happen if she
did something before she did it.

I looked at that paragraph for a while. Then I wrote,

The building manager's daughter was so glad about her father forgiving her that she promised to think ahead from now on.

My dad took the pen again.

Which made him very proud of her.

I slid over and gave my dad a hug. "I think it's a really good book," I whispered.

"Me, too," he whispered back. "I think it'll probably be a best seller."

On the way to school Thursday, Margaret asked me how it was going with the substitute.

"Not so good," I told her. Then, before she could give me any more bad ideas like copying Lilly, I told her about my dad getting mad at me for a while. Instead of telling me everything I did wrong, Margaret surprised me. She started to cry!

"What's the matter?" And then she surprised me even more: she wiped her tears on my jacket even though it was probably crawling with germs.

"My father can't come this month. The actress

in his decongestant commercial broke her foot. So now she can't go running through her garden saying how great it is to breathe freely again. They've got to find another actress and start all over."

"I'm really sorry," I said. And I was. Margaret and Mitchell looked forward to their father's visits all month. It was all they could talk about.

"You're so lucky," she sniffed. "And you don't even know it!"

"What are you talking about? Why am I lucky?"

"Because you see your father every day."

"But you're lucky, too," I said. "When your father comes it's for a whole week. You do everything with him. He doesn't work when he visits, and it's like a vacation every time. My dad's always working."

"I guess," said Margaret.

"And you get to stay with him in his hotel and call room service and take the wrappings off the cups in the bathroom. And the toilet has a little strip over it that says 'Sanitized for Your Protection'—you love that!"

Margaret nodded and brightened up a little.

"And sometimes you get to go to Hollywood, California, and watch them make commercials! I think that's lucky. And one day, your dad might even let you be in one!"

We sat there for a minute, breathing the bus air and thinking about who was lucky.

"I guess we both are," Margaret said at last. "Just different kinds of lucky."

Except I wasn't so lucky once I got into school.

During math, Mrs. Nagel wrote a hard problem on the board and then asked if anyone knew the solution to it. I raised my hand and told her the answer.

If my real teacher were there, he would have tapped his nose and then pointed at me, smiling.

This means, *You got that right on the nose! Good thinking!*

Instead, Mrs. Nagel said, "That's correct, Clementine. But I didn't ask for the answer. I just asked if anyone knew it."

Which was practically the same thing as saying "You are never going to be a successful student."

Then she wiped the board clean, and I bet she wiped so hard she practically rubbed the green right off.

In language arts, she made us read our journal entries out loud.

"But our teacher doesn't make us read them out loud," I told her.

"But Mr. D'Matz isn't here," she reminded me. Which I had not forgotten. "So today we will." So I had to read my journal entry, which was about why I love bricks so much, and now that's not a secret anymore.

Mrs. Nagel was mean to me three more times. The only good thing was that I finally figured it out: why I was getting in so much trouble. I raised my hand and told her I needed to visit the principal.

She said All right, which probably meant, *Good, now I can get a little work done with the successful students.* Which made me even madder. I stomped down the hall so hard I probably broke the school basement, and I didn't care about that.

Mrs. Rice took one look at my face when I walked in and said, "Do you want to tell me what's bothering you today?"

"Not yet," I said. "Do you like tattoos?"

"Not too much. Do you?"

"Yes," I said. I took a deep breath. "Okay, now I want to tell you. I can't guess Mrs. Nagel's rules. She has different ones from my teacher and she doesn't tell them until it's too late and I'm already in trouble. Which isn't fair. So I was just wondering if you could make my teacher come back a little early. Like today. Could you call him

up and tell him to skip all that getting-ready-for-Egypt stuff for the rest of the week? He doesn't want to be there anyway."

"I'm sorry, Clementine, but no. I just spoke with him, by the way, and he's having a wonderful time."

I folded my arms across my chest and felt my face getting madder and madder.

"Clementine, do you think it's possible Mrs. Nagel feels the same way you do? That she can't guess the rules? It's hard to be a substitute. To learn the new rules of a school. Do you think maybe you should help her out by explaining how your class does things?"

"No," I growled. "I do not."

Mrs. Rice just sat there looking at me until finally she hypnotized my mouth to say, "Okay, fine, maybe *someone* should."

I looked at her hard when I said "someone," but she only looked back at me harder.

I shook my head. "Maybe a sixth grader. Not me."

Mrs. Rice leaned back in her chair. "Well, that's too bad. I think you'd do a good job of it." She stood up. "Let's go back to your classroom. Mr. D'Matz asked me to let you all know how much he liked his Good Luck cards. He also asked me to tell the class what he's been doing this week." She handed me her dictionary. "If you look up 'mummification' you can help explain what he's learning about."

I looked up the word, and then we went back to my classroom.

Mrs. Rice told everyone how much Mr. D'Matz appreciated our nice cards. She said he was having a wonderful week and that today he'd learned more about mummification. "And now Clementine will explain what that means."

"First they scoop out the guy's guts with a big spoon," I said. "Then they go for the brains through his nose. If the mummy starts sneezing when they do this, there are brains flying every-where. They have to scrape them off the ceiling with a shovel—"

Beside me, Mrs. Rice cleared her throat.

"All right, no. I guess that doesn't happen a lot.

But it's pretty disgusting. And besides," I said, "under all the wrappings, those mummies are *naked*!"

Mrs. Rice sighed a huge sigh. "Thank you, Clementine, for that enlightening look at mummification."

When I got home from school, I put the twenty-two dollars in my pocket and started for the top floor.

"Hi-Mrs.-Jacobi-I'm-sorry-I-sold-private-giveaway-stuff-here's-your-money-do-you-want-it-back?"

Mrs. Jacobi just looked at me like I was crazy. "I love my place mats," she said. "I don't want my money back."

At the next floor it was the same thing. And the next. And the next. Everybody looked at me like I was crazy. Everybody was happy with what they'd bought. Nobody wanted their money back. I went to Margaret and Mitchell's apartment last, because Alan doesn't show up until four o'clock.

Mitchell answered the door. "Hi, Clementine!" he said. He had a huge grin on his face.

"Is Alan here?" I asked.

"Nope!" he cried. His grin got even bigger.

"Why not?"

Mitchell's face nearly split in two. "You know that pipe you sold him? The one he said was just like one he lost? Well, it *was* his. He hadn't lost it—my mom had thrown it away! So now he's mad at her, and he's not coming over. Thanks, Clementine!"

Usually when someone thanks me for something, I feel good. Not this time. But I said, "You're welcome," anyway.

Then I realized something—I still had the money for my mom's present! "We have to go back to the art store now," I told Mitchell.

"Okay," he said.

This is a good thing about Mitchell—he never asks why, he just does stuff for me. If I'd asked Margaret, she would have asked me a hundred questions and then told me a hundred reasons why my idea was stupid and she had a better one.

Not Mitchell. He just says Okay. If I ever have a boyfriend, which I will not, it might be him.

"Let's bring your brother," Mitchell said. This is another good thing about him—he likes my brother. And my brother likes him.

So we went down to my apartment and got Scallion and strapped him into the stroller. Mitchell leaned over. "Stroller derby?" he asked.

My brother just shrieked, which is how he says yes when he's too excited to speak. He shrieks a lot around Mitchell.

Mitchell took off with my brother, running as fast as he could without actually flattening anybody on the street. My brother kept shrieking the whole time because he loves stroller derby so

much, and because he likes to hear his voice shake when they hit the sidewalk bumps. I had to run to keep up, and we got there in just a few minutes.

Inside, I slapped my money on the counter, out of breath.

"You're back," the clerk said. Then he asked me how my great-aunt Rose was.

"I don't know," I told him. "I haven't seen her this week. But I guess she's normal." Then I asked him how *his* great-aunt was.

"I don't know," he said. "I haven't seen mine this week, either. But I guess she's normal, too."

Then we were all done being polite, so the clerk wrapped up the art supplies organizer. I strapped the package onto the seat beneath my brother, and we headed home.

"No stroller derby, this time," I warned Mitchell.

Mitchell and my brother looked at me like they were both too heartbroken to speak. But I stayed firm. "Sorry," I said. "Not with something so valuable in the stroller." This is called Being Responsible.

My mother had left a note:

> Gone to deliver my drawings.
> Dad's out back with the masons.

Daikon radish was conked out from all that shrieking, so I strollered him out back and sat down on the bench next to my dad.

He lifted my brother onto his lap. "What's in the bag?" he asked.

I pulled out the wooden box. "For Mom. She's going to love it. For her art supplies. She's going to love it, don't you think?"

My dad took the box. "Wow," he said. "She's

going to love it all right. But we talked about this. You know you don't have to—"

"I know," I said. "I just got thinking about how happy it would make her. I wanted to see her 'Wow! I must be dreaming!' face."

Dad smiled. "I like it when she makes that face, too. Well, I guess it makes it better then—what you did. It's a good reason . . . wanting to make someone happy."

"Is everyone in the building still mad at each other?" I asked.

He nodded. "Let's just say the air in the elevator was a little frosty today."

"They wanted their giveaways to be private," I said.

My dad nodded again. "That's why they were in shopping bags."

"But I didn't know that."

"I know."

"I like to know the rules ahead of time," I said.

"I understand," my dad said.

Then we were quiet for a while, watching the masons finish the wall. Which gave me a good idea. I told it to my dad.

"I don't see why not," he said. "There are enough bricks left over and enough money in the building improvements budget."

So we asked the masons if they could build a little brick wall around the charity collection area and they said, Sure.

When it was done, my dad and I built a wooden cover for it with a little door on the top for people to drop their giveaways into. I made a sign that said

PRIVATE!
No taking stuff out and selling it!

Then I decorated the sign with SORRYs and put in the two dollars I had left from what I sold.

"That should take care of it," my dad said.

"That should make everyone in the building happy."

Almost everyone.

I asked my dad if we could eat our dinner up on the roof. "And play Life? And could Margaret and

Mitchell come, too?" I explained to him about their father not coming this weekend and about Margaret crying. "And could you be a substitute father for her?"

"A substitute? I don't know. Margaret seems a little . . . particular about things. I don't know if I could figure out her rules."

"Well . . . I guess you shouldn't worry about Margaret's rules. Just be your regular, own kind of dad."

"Okay," my dad said, "I'll do it."

We brought my brother inside, and I called up Margaret and asked if she and Mitchell could have pizza up on the roof with us.

"Thank goodness!" she said. "My mother's making an 'I'm sorry' dinner for Alan. Meat loaf. Extra onions. And he's probably going to kiss her!"

Just then, my mom walked in looking kind of

droopy. She held up her drawings. "He didn't like them. 'Not scriggly enough,' he said. 'Too whooshy.'"

I told her I thought they were the perfect amount of scriggly and not too whooshy at all. "But I have something that will make you feel better!"

I made her sit down. "Close your eyes!" I said, and then I got the deluxe art supplies organizer and put it on her lap. When she opened her eyes, she got so excited she couldn't finish her sentences, which is usually a bad sign, but not then.

"Look at all the . . . for my brushes . . . And it has a . . . So now he can't get into . . . !" And all the time she was making the "Wow! I must be dreaming!" face, which was so pretty I'm going to make a drawing of it some day.

My brother woke up then, and we all waited while he said hi to his feet and then showed them to us as if we'd never met them before. Then my mom scooped him onto her lap and gave him a couple of the empty cookie tins. "It's your lucky day, too," she told him. "You get presents, too!" My brother grinned and began to bang the cookie tins together. Then my mom looked over at me. "Oh, wait. Clementine, would you like some of them?"

And right away, without even thinking about it, I said, "No, he can have them all. I don't mind!" And that was the truth! My dad winked at me and

that made his face look so nice that I am going to do a drawing of that some day, too.

Then we ordered two pizzas and we picked up Margaret and Mitchell on the fifth floor and we all went up to the roof. We didn't play Life, though, because we had so many other things to do up there.

The sun was setting, and I listed every color I could see in the clouds over Boston. I counted thirty-three.

Next, Mitchell pointed to where Fenway Park was. He told us about every ball that was belted out of the park this season—who hit it, how far it went, who won.

Then we turned the lamp onto Margaret, and she acted out every one of her father's commercials. My dad clapped like crazy and said, "I'm going to *buy that product!*" after each one. This made Margaret smile so big, her teeth bracelets sparkled in the lamplight.

Even Spinach did something up there: he shrieked whenever Mitchell winked at him.

As we were packing up our stuff to go back inside, Mitchell asked me about my teacher. "So. Did he go camping?"

"He's not going now. He's not going to break

his promise. He didn't want to go anyway."

"Well, that's good that he changed his mind."

"He didn't exactly change his mind." I explained about the letter to the judges.

Mitchell stopped and stared at me. "You wrote all those terrible things I told you about Beans McCloud? But what if he reads it? Your teacher?"

"He won't. It's a letter to the judges."

"Are you sure?"

"Of course. I'm sure." But all of a sudden—okay, fine—I wasn't.

Back in our apartment, my parents went into my brother's room to tuck him into bed. I went into their room and opened up my dad's book. I found the page where he had written about how proud the building manager was because his daughter promised she was going to think ahead from now on. And I wrote:

But she might not be so good at this.

CHAPTER

I I

On Friday morning, I woke up a little bit excited: today was the last day I'd have to put up with Mrs. Nagel. I felt a little worried, too, as if something bad was about to happen, but I didn't know what it was.

I found out at school.

"We'll leave for the statehouse after lunch," Mrs. Nagel announced. She picked up a notice. "It says the ceremony starts with the letter reading at one o'clock."

"What do you mean, letter reading?" I asked. "Out loud?"

"I don't know," she answered. "Letter reading;

Winner announcement; Speech. That's all it says."

Which gave me a heart attack. All morning I just sat there with my chest squeezing me so hard I was frozen in my seat. I was so quiet I didn't have to hear a single "Clementine-you-need-to-pay-attention!" which was a new record for me. That is the good news about heart attacks, I guess.

And then it was time to go. While everyone was getting jackets and backpacks, I just stood in the corner.

"Are you all right, Clementine?" Mrs. Nagel asked.

"I'm having a heart attack," I told her. "I think I should go home."

She squinted at me for a minute. "I doubt that's it. You're probably just excited about visiting the statehouse."

So I had to walk out with Mrs. Nagel, and when I took a seat on the bus, she sat down beside me.

"I'm glad we have this chance to talk," she said when the bus started up. "I'm afraid you and I didn't have a very successful week."

I decided that since I was probably going to die soon, I might as well tell her the truth. "I couldn't guess any of your rules," I told her.

"What do you mean?"

I took a big breath. "Your rules are different

from my teacher's. It took me a long time to learn those, but I did. So when I saw those apple slices on Monday, I remembered our 'Feed the hamsters first' rule, but I didn't guess about your 'Don't touch it because it's a science experiment' rule. When you put that math problem on the board yesterday, I remembered our 'Magic zero place-holder' rule, but I didn't guess about your 'Don't say the answer out loud' rule. When you handed out that paper the first day, I remembered our 'Put your name in the upper right–hand corner' rule, but I didn't guess about your 'Don't make a mark on it' rule."

I took another big breath. "I like to know the rules about things first. Before I can make a mistake."

"Oh." Mrs. Nagel was quiet for a minute. Then she said, "That makes sense. I wish we'd talked about this on Monday."

"Me too," I said. "But I didn't know what the

problem was on Monday." Then I showed her my arm reminder.

Mrs. Nagel studied it for a while, and then she took out a pen and wrote the same thing down on her arm, too! I am not even kidding about that! SOMETIMES YOU HAVE TO FIGURE OUT THE PROBLEM BEFORE YOU CAN FIGURE OUT THE SOLUTION. "Thank you for that good advice," she said.

I just stared at her arm for a minute. Then I remembered my manners. "You're welcome."

"And how about this?" she said. "If your teacher wins the trip, I'll be here for the rest of the year. So on Monday morning, would you tell me about *your* classroom rules? Because I don't know any of *them*."

I said, Sure, even though I knew my

teacher was not going to win that trip. Thinking about that made my heart attack hurt worse. By the time we got to the statehouse, I was practically dead from it.

The other two classes were already in the lobby. One was a group of high schoolers, standing around butting each other with their shoulders. The other was a kindergarten class. They were butting each other with their shoulders, too, but they weren't standing around, because most of

them had been knocked to the floor. Before our class could get going with the shoulder-butting, it was time to go into the auditorium.

First, the high schoolers filed down and sat on the right-hand side. Next went the kindergartners, and they went over to the left. The sitting-down part didn't work very well for them, though.

They were so little that any time they sat back, the seats sprang closed, snapping at them like alligators in a frog pond. Things got a little crazy

for a while, with nineteen little kids collapsing into the seats and screaming like they were being gobbled up. Which they might have been.

"Good grief," I heard Mrs. Rice whisper to Mrs. Nagel. "Let's hope our kids are heavy enough! Otherwise the PTA is going to have a canary!"

Finally, someone got nineteen law books and weighed down the kindergartners' laps with them. Then our class went in and sat right in the middle.

In front of us, at a long table with a sign that said JUDGING COMMITTEE, were four people. One of them wore a badge and a serious face, which meant he was the boss.

Behind them sat the three teachers vying for the award. I kept my eyes turned away so I wouldn't have to see Mr. D'Matz.

The boss judge stood up. "We will hear one student letter about each teacher," he said. "Then we'll announce our final decision."

The kindergarten teacher went first. She beckoned to a tiny girl who was missing all her front teeth. She looked relieved to be away from her snapping seat, probably because she couldn't bite back. Since kindergartners are too young to write letters, she just told the judges why her teacher should be the winner.

"My teather ith the betht one," she started. After that, I had no idea what she was saying, and I don't think the judges did either, although they kept smiling and nodding.

Next was the high school teacher's turn. A boy with purple hair spikes got up and fake yawned to

show he wasn't nervous about reading his letter.

I didn't understand much that he said either, even though he had all his teeth. There was some stuff about achievement tests and some stuff about academic atmosphere and some words even bigger than that. I was pretty sure he was making them up.

The judges smiled and nodded through his letter, too, though.

Then Mr. D'Matz stood up. The judges handed him a big envelope, and he pulled a sheet of paper from it. "Clementine, would you please come up and read your letter?"

From my seat, I shook my head *no* and arrow-eyed him hard.

He nodded *yes* and arrow-eyed me harder.

I looked back at him even harder.

I didn't use stingray eyes, of course, but it wouldn't have mattered. Because then he looked back at me with his best trick: laser eyes!

Laser eyes are the most powerful eyes of all. They hypnotized me to stand up and walk over to the podium. Mr. D'Matz handed me my letter and I took it. And I started to read.

"'I have to tell you some things about my teacher. If you go camping with him, and you have to have beans . . .'"

And then I sneaked a look at him—my teacher.

Because I wanted to see him one last time before he hated me for life.

And when I found his face, it was shining with a happy smile that said, *I'm going to Egypt and Clementine is helping me.*

The paper fell out of my hands. The judge boss picked it up and held it out to me.

I pushed it away and shook my head. "It's okay," I told him. "I don't need it. I know what I want to tell you about my teacher." And then I started over.

But not with the things I had written on Monday.

"If you go camping with him and you have to have beans, you will be lucky. Because even if you've never made them, it will be okay. My teacher would never say, 'How come you don't know how to make beans? I taught you how to do that last week!' No. He would say something like, 'Say, I see you're planning to make some beans. I know you'll be successful at that because you're good at so many things. You'll probably start by opening the can, then you'll get a clean pot.' And without you even knowing it, he will teach you how to make beans. And here is the tricky part: somehow, you will think you learned it all by yourself! Plus, you'll think making beans is the most interesting thing in the world to do, because my teacher makes everything interesting. Even things that other people might think are weird!

"And every morning when you go to school—I mean when you go camping with him—you'll be excited to see what he's got planned for the day. And when it's time to go home, you'll be a little bit sorry, because you've had a really good time. But you'll know that's okay, because he's got lots of excellent projects planned and he'll be there the next day. And—"

I felt a hand on my shoulder and looked up.

Mrs. Rice nodded down at me. "Thank you, Clementine," she said, as if I was all finished.

"But there's more," I said. "I want to tell them more."

"I know," she said. "But that's enough for now." Then she led me back to my seat, which was good, because my heart attack had gotten to my

eyes and made them a little blurry.

The judges got up and walked over to . . . my teacher. They smiled and shook his hand. Then they walked over to the other teachers and smiled and shook their hands, too. Then the four judges came back to their table, and the boss one picked up the microphone.

"The winner of this year's Great Adventure for Teachers program is . . ."

And right then I knew they were going to say my teacher's name, because of what I said about him. Which made me feel really, really sad and really, really happy, too. Which must have confused my ears, because what I heard was: ". . . Miss Gladys Huffman!"

The kindergarten teacher must have heard that, too—she walked to the podium with a huge I-can't-believe-it's-me! grin on her face. The kindergartners jumped up and started clapping like crazy. This was not such a good idea because the law books all fell off and the seats started snapping at them again.

"Thank-you-very-much-I-couldn't-have-done-it-without-my-wonderful-students," Miss Gladys Huffman said in a hurry into the microphone. "And now I think I better go rescue them!"

And that was the end of the program.

My teacher came over to our class and knelt down in front of me. "Thank you so much for that outstanding letter of recommendation, Clementine."

"But you didn't win," I said. "I'm sorry about that." Which suddenly I actually was! Okay, fine—sort of.

"Don't be," he said. "I'm not."

"You're not?"

"I'm not," he repeated. "I really did want to

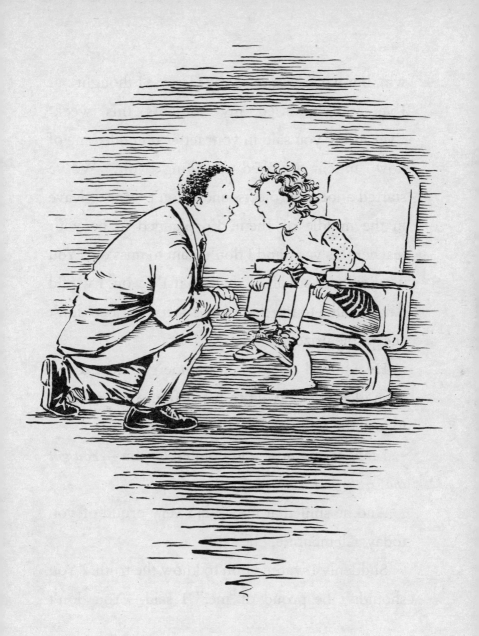

win, but when you read your letter, I thought . . . I've really missed my students this week. Everything you said in your letter reminded me of how much I liked teaching you. We've started a lot of projects, and I don't want to leave in the middle of them. I'd planned to be your teacher this year, and I don't want to miss out. You were right about all of that. So if I'd won, I would have wanted to tell them I was sorry, but I couldn't accept the prize."

He nodded over to the kindergarten teacher. "I'm glad they gave it to her. I figure an archaeological dig will feel like a vacation to her!"

I tapped my nose and pointed to him—*You got that right on the nose! Good thinking!*

And he smiled at me. "I am very proud of you today, Clementine," he said.

Suddenly I wanted him to know the truth. "You shouldn't be proud of me," I said. "You don't know what was really in my letter." .

"Yes I do," he said. "I read them all this morning."

"Oh, no. You couldn't have read my letter," I told him.

Mr. D'Matz raised his eyebrows at me. "'The smell of his socks could peel the wrapping off a mummy. If he walked by, the Great Sphinx would keel over.'"

"Then . . . how come . . . how did you know I would . . . ?"

"Do you remember the story about the mother bird?"

I didn't make the here-we-go-again face, because just then I wanted to hear that story. But Mr. D'Matz didn't tell it. Instead, he shook my hand and said, "I knew you could fly, Clementine. And I knew that you would."

As I sat there, shaking my teacher's hand, my heart attack went away. And you will not believe what happened next! I felt a prickling all over my skin.

And you know what that was?

Feathers!

Okay, fine. It was goose bumps.

Sara Pennypacker is also the author of *The Talented Clementine*; *Stuart's Cape* and *Stuart Goes to School*; *Dumbstruck*; and *Pierre in Love*. She was a painter before becoming a writer, and has two absolutely fabulous children who are now grown. Sara lives on Cape Cod in Massachusetts.

Marla Frazee illustrated the second book in this series, *The Talented Clementine*. She is the author and illustrator of many picture books as well, including *Walk On!*, *Santa Claus the World's Number One Toy Expert*, and *Roller Coaster*, and illustrated *The Seven Silly Eaters* and *Everywhere Babies*. Marla works in a small backyard cabin under an avocado tree in Pasadena, California.